The Ruby Slippers

By

Tracy Baines

First Published 2016

Author: Tracy Baines

www.tracybaines.co.uk

ISBN-13:978-1523974184
ISBN-10:1523974184

ABOUT THIS COLLECTION

These uplifting stories have previously been published in *Woman's Weekly*, *My Weekly*, *Take A Break*, *Best* and *The People's Friend.* This is the first time they have all been brought together in one place.
These heart-warming stories explore the everyday relationships of families, couples and friends. How, with a huge amount of love and large dashings of humour, we find the strength and wherewithal to get through the complicated tapestry of life.

Ruby Slippers
Angie's marriage is dull and predictable. Phil hardly notices her any more. Can a pair of shoes revive their relationship, or will she regret her expensive purchase?
Table for Two
Had Jules made the right decision all those years ago? Would a cosy, intimate dinner with her ex lead to regrets?
Hilary's Handbag
Just what docs Hilary keep in her beautiful patchwork handbag?

Ruby Slippers

Small beads of sweat formed on Angie's forehead as she passed her credit card to the assistant but she'd managed to stop her hands from shaking. Did she look too desperate? In her panic she thought she heard the card gasp as the extra weight was placed on it.

Sitting on the bus, homeward bound, she tried not to think of the money. She cradled the black glossy bag as tenderly as a child, the red cord handles threaded around her fingers to prevent its escape. She looked at the tired grey faces around her. Did she look guilty?

"Well, what do you think?" She held one up, trophy like, for Phil to admire.

Phil, stretched out on the sofa, lowered his newspaper just enough to show willing.

"I thought only ladies of the night wore red shoes," he said, before resuming his intense study of the TV guide.

It wasn't the reaction she'd expected. Not that she'd anticipated anything but a grunt and 'very nice, Ange'. She put the shoe back into the box.

"Aren't you thinking of red lights, Phil?"

"Red lights, red shoes. Same thing." He folded the paper in half, dropped it on the floor, picked up the remote and flicked on the TV.

Angie persevered. "I was thinking more of Dorothy's ruby slippers."

Eyes fixed to screen. Ronnie O'Sullivan going for the break.

"Who's Dorothy?"

She sat on the arm of the chair.

"Judy Garland? *The Wizard of Oz*?"

He winced as the white bounced blindly off the cushion.

"Judy and Dorothy who?"

Angie sighed. "I'll get on with making dinner."

She returned the shoes to the bag and left them on the bottom stair.

Half an hour later she presented him with sausage and mash on a tray accompanied by a couple of cans of beer. He didn't have to move from the sofa all night. She knew he wouldn't anyway. Angie ate alone at the kitchen table.

She silently cleared the plates away, stuck her head around the door to say she was having a bath. Another grunt. Why did she bother?

The shoebox sat on the bed, making a dent in the duvet that made them look as if they were being presented on a giant cushion. A pair of glass slippers for Cinderella. She gently eased off the lid, teased back the tissue that cocooned them and took each one out, turning them about in her hands, admiring the craftsmanship. The most beautiful things she'd ever seen, the most beautiful things she'd ever owned – a work of art. The ruby red silk was perfect, the small diamante fastenings faultless, the heels exquisitely crafted, finely chiselled spikes. Not the usual cheap shoes she bought for herself which lasted a few months and were more economical to throw away than to get re-heeled. She felt a frisson of excitement run through her body. It was like caressing a new lover. She put them in the box, folding the tissue over them as if wrapping a child in a cradle, and went to the bathroom. She poured bubble bath from a jumbo sized container into the running water and rescued a couple of fresh towels from the airing cupboard on the landing, searching for at least one that wasn't hard to the touch. Soaking in the steam, she dreamed of scented oils and outsized fluffy towels. If only. She laid back and tried not to think of the price of the shoes.

Later, she rummaged around in the wardrobe for something suitable to wear with the shoes. Black, navy and every shade of grey hung from the rail. She dragged out her trusty black dress, long sleeves, scoop neck. Classic, serviceable. She held the hanger up to the light and held the shoes beneath.

She found a suspender belt, took out the stockings purchased when paying for the ruby slippers. Tights wouldn't do the shoes justice. Effort was called for. She slid the shoes on to stockinged feet, stretching her legs out, turning them this way and that, pointing her toes. She stood and looked in the mirror – her legs were still good, the shoes accentuated their shapeliness – it was her torso, round as a bumblebee that let her down. Well, that could be changed. Given time. She closed her eyes, clicked her heels three times.

"There's no place like home," she whispered, "there's no place like home, there's no place like home." Slowly, she opened her eyes again. She wasn't in Kansas, she remained in suburbia, stuck firmly in her rut. This was no dream, there was no fantasy land to escape to. Reality stung her like never before. It seeped into her pores, bored itself into her capillaries and misery pumped through her body. She wasn't Dorothy – just Angie from accounts, Angela Porter from Laurel Drive; Phil's wife.

She looked again in the mirror. Where would she wear such shoes? What special occasions did she attend these days? They were too vampish for the staff party. And if she wasn't going to wear them there was no point in keeping them, was there? At least she knew that if she couldn't live with the guilt she had twenty-eight days to redeem herself. Perhaps a better deal than the confessional offered. She pushed the receipt to the back of her bedside drawer.

She slipped off the shoes, balanced them on outstretched palms and regarded them. A tingle of excitement stretched and yawned within her. She was reminded of her first pair of patent shoes, bought for a winter wedding she'd attended. Mother had bought her a crimson coat with black buttons and matching velvet collar and cuffs. Gran said she looked like one of the royals – Angie feared it was Charles. She'd loved those shoes – so shiny that the lights reflected in them. She had slept with them on her pillow for days, wanting to lay all night and adore them. The last thing she saw before she closed her eyes. She wondered whether to do that now. Would Phil even notice a competitor vying for her adoration?

She placed them under the bed.

That night she dreamed of shoes. Tiny shoes that she had to force her feet into. Different styles, heels and flats, her white flesh spilling over the edges, her toes being curled and pushed painfully into the point. The harder she pushed the larger her feet seemed to grow.

The dream was with her when she woke the next morning and she checked her feet, reassured by their familiarity. As she put on her make-up she picked up the framed wedding photo on her dressing table. The advent of colour film had made no difference. The groom wore black, the bride white, the only splash of colour in the portrait coming from the flowers in her bouquet.

Lunch break, she dashed through the rain, called in the florists and bought two mixed bouquets. Water gathered in huge puddles and soaked into her suede boots as she hurried through the streets and brought back thoughts of patent shoes and Emily Snape's party.

Emily Snape who'd spilled cherryade on her, that had soaked through her cotton dress and left a raspberry coloured stain on her white socks. She remembered watching as the liquid magically dribbled off her patent shoes.

On the fourth day she stopped on the way home from work and bought steak; plucked vibrant coloured vegetables, green and orange, from the display. When she arrived home she set the table, rescuing the linen tablecloth from the recesses of the kitchen cupboard, lighting candles, dimming the lights. The plump red steak sat waiting on a white plate, oozing blood, before she laid it gingerly into the pan. It spat and sizzled, filling the kitchen with rich aromas. She called Phil through when it was on the table.

"Are we celebrating something, Ange?"

She shook her head.

A veil of panic slid over his face. "I've forgotten something. Haven't I?"

"No," she said. "Nothing forgotten." Smiling, chewing, she watched as he cut into his steak. Enjoyment replaced his uneasiness. Not an expression you got with ready meals from the microwave.

"We don't need an excuse do we?" she said.

"No, I don't suppose we do."

They sat for a while when they'd finished eating, drinking wine, talking about nothing in particular. He helped her clear the table, squeezed up close against her as she stood by the sink. "Thanks, Ange."

Saturday she was bored. She moved things around in the lounge.

Phil came in, sat in the chair, flicked on the TV, then stopped, looked around.

"You've changed something."

"Yes," she said.

He nodded with approval.

"Nice," he said. "Yeh. It's nice." He patted the settee. "Got time for a cuddle?"

The trouble she got into over those patent shoes, saved only for special occasions. She sneaked them out of the house on the way to school, in the dark recesses of the brown canvas bag she slung over her shoulder. She had felt like a princess. Running around the playground, skipping, climbing the frame, she had scuffed the toes. She was devastated to find they were merely grey canvas underneath. She tried to stretch the patent back, painting it with thick school glue to stop more damage. But it was too late. It peeled away like blister skin and she began to pick at it like scabs.

She bought towels in the sale, russet and buttermilk, stacked them on the bathroom shelves. Honey coloured bath oils in gold topped glass bottles flanked the windowsill. Each night she lay back in her luxury bubbles, drinking wine, thinking about the shoes. She still had fourteen days. There was no rush.

And after each bath, after lathering herself with perfumed

body lotion, Angie walked in front of the mirror, posing, learning to look with a keener eye. Yes, her legs were still good – and was her eyesight playing games or had she lost a few pounds these past couple of weeks? She paraded nightly, in her ruby slippers and all the time Phil sat downstairs watching moving pictures. She didn't call him. She wasn't doing this for him.

On day fifteen she had her hair coloured, chestnut shot with autumn gold, a fresher style; sleek and glossy.

She'd picked up one of the gossipy magazines laid around the salon and discovered that red increased your appetite. She considered painting the bedroom walls a deep crimson, she'd seen it in the home magazines, it could look rather luxurious with the right accessories – but there would be no on and off switch and that might get tiresome. No, it would have to be something more subtle.

It was on the twenty-third day that Angie decided to return the shoes. She couldn't bear the thought of what everyday wear and tear would do to her beautiful ruby slippers. It was impossible to think of them worn and shabby. Unworn they were perfect, magical.

One last time she carefully wrapped them in the tissue paper. She'd expected to feel sad but was surprised to feel a rush of energy she hadn't felt for a long time.

On the way to the shoe shop she called in the portrait photographers.

A week later she'd seen the proofs, made her choice and asked for it to be printed on canvas. They called her when it was ready. She ordered a taxi – she wouldn't risk bringing it home on the bus. The canvas was wrapped in thick brown paper, tied crossways with black ribbon woven with the name of the studio. She clutched it to her as she had the shoes those few weeks ago.

Phil was home. Surprised to see her in a taxi. He followed her into the lounge, curious as she unwrapped the parcel. Angie propped it against the mantle and stepped back to admire it, slipping her arm around Phil's waist and leaning on his chest. He smelt of soap and fresh air.

He didn't speak for a while.

"But it's just a pair of shoes," he said.

"Yes," said Angie, her hand on his heart. "It's just a pair of shoes."

Perfect

I knew she'd be late. That was just her style, to keep me waiting, make me agitated. Although, how she could still have that effect on me after all these years I can't imagine. Funny how the memories come flooding back at the mention of a name. The girl that had taken the booking had said that she specifically asked for me, which made me curious from the start. Why make contact after all these years? I knew she was back in town – I just wondered how long it would be before she came to call.

People talk a lot when they're in a beauty salon, it's like the hairdressers. Small chit-chat about nothing in particular – 'are you going somewhere special', you know the sort of thing – with a bit of gossip thrown in on the side.

I hadn't seen Carol Stevens since we left school over twenty years ago and that had suited me fine. Her cousin was a regular customer so I often heard of her latest acquisitions – the big house, the flash car, exotic holidays – and it made me feel, in some perverse way, that I was still in competition with her. I felt all the old insecurities and inadequacies kicking in, so much so that even the staff had noticed that I wasn't my usual self today. Too busy straightening already straight towels and pictures. The mirrors gleamed and the floor shone. I snapped at the staff when there was no call for it. I wanted things to be perfect. I looked at my watch. She was over thirty minutes late, maybe she wasn't going to come after all. Typical. I was just about to give up on her when she came breezing into the salon, all smiles and teeth, Gucci handbag swinging from her arm.

"Oh Lindy," she gasped breathily. "Sorry I'm late. Traffic – you know how it is. I left my car out front." She pointed to a gleaming silver Mercedes sports. "It'll be safe there won't it?"

"Of course," I said. That was probably the reason she was late, waiting for a space right outside the salon. "It'll be fine there for an hour and we won't be that long." I managed a smile as I took her coat. Rumour was rife as to why she was back in town. "I'd heard you were back home."

"Only visiting," she said rather too quickly. "I'm staying with Mum for a while, catching up on old times, old friends – like you."

She kissed the air both sides of my cheeks, then held my hands and stood back to look me up and down.

"My, how you've changed, Lindy. You've really made the best of what you've got, haven't you? Must be one of the benefits of working here."

"I don't work here, Carol. I own it." I was surprised at the pleasure I felt in telling her; a little tremble of delight shooting through my body.

She let my hands drop and seemed to be a little flustered.

"Well, I did hear that somewhere but I didn't think for a minute it would be true. Did you win the lottery or something, I mean it's really rather swish isn't it?" She looked around the salon, her greedy eyes taking in the surroundings; the calm creams, luxurious suede furnishings, the huge vases of lilies that graced the tables.

"Thanks," I said, still smiling at her. "But it's all down to hard work, Carol; that, and going without." Not that she'd understand anything about that. Carol had never had to work hard – there was always someone willing to do her homework for her, lend her a tie so she didn't get detention, give her their lunch money because she'd spent hers on make-up. She used her looks to make life go exactly the way she wanted; and it always seemed to work.

I showed her into one of the treatment rooms.

"If you just strip down to your underwear and lie on the bed," I told her. "I'll get everything ready and be back in a minute or two. One of the girls will get you a drink. Would you like tea or coffee?"

"Have you any mineral water?" she asked.

"Still or sparkling?"

"Sparkling, of course."

"Of course," I muttered, closing the door behind me. I

got one of the girls to take her a drink and I went into the preparation room, wishing our paths had never crossed again.

I'd met her when we moved because of my dad's job and I had to start a new school. The teacher, in her wisdom, sat me next to Carol because she thought she'd be good for me. And I suppose she was in a way. Everyone wanted to be Carol's friend – she was the coolest girl in the school. We were chalk and cheese of course. I was the 'don't fancy yours much' friend. Hardly competition.

But little things she said and did would quietly eat away at me until I felt that without her friendship no one would like me. She couldn't bear it if I was complimented in any way. She couldn't compete in the classroom so instead, she would undermine my appearance, remarking on my too big nose or my too thin arms and gradually I became awkward, unsure of myself, focussing on my bad points, of which there were many.

I could never understand why. She had everything a girl could want in bucket loads. She had a stunning figure, beautiful skin and long, auburn hair that cascaded about her shoulders. I always felt drab and mousey next to her perfection. Nevertheless, Carol was never satisfied unless she had everything.

As we grew older she developed a more vindictive edge to her competitiveness. The worst betrayal of all was when she discovered that I fancied Colin Peters. I silently worshipped him, too shy to let him know. She dumped her boyfriend like a shot when she found out and went all out for him. When she succeeded, she paraded him in front of me like a trophy. It still hurt after all these years, the indignation that had made me throw a protective shell around myself and I had never really got close to, or confided in, anyone since. I never wanted to be that vulnerable again.

I put the wax in the machine to warm. It would be so easy to make it too hot. Even easier to make her eyebrows disappear altogether. I laughed to myself at my wickedness. But I couldn't do it, not to her, and especially not now. Not if everything I'd heard was true.

I returned to the room. She was laid out on the bed, auburn curls cascading around her head, designer silk undies of palest peach upon her slender, tanned body – no doubt finely honed on some Caribbean beach. I sighed at the unfairness of it all. She was still beautiful. Perfect, even.

"I'll start with your eyebrows and upper lip," I told her. "Then your lower legs and do your bikini line last. Okay?"

"You're the expert," she said. "I'm in your hands now."

And she was, at long last, totally vulnerable to me. The temptation was almost irresistible. I began to make the usual polite conversation. Asked how her parents were, where she lived now, what she was doing. I wasn't surprised when she was vague and tried to skim over her replies. She didn't seem too keen on rubbing my face in her achievements now.

She deftly changed the subject and began to chat about the old days at school.

"We had such fun then, didn't we, Lindy?"

"Sometimes," I replied. I concentrated on smoothing the wax carefully upon her face.

"Can you remember how we fell out over Colin Peters? You wouldn't speak to me for days."

"I remember that," I said, coldly, gently easing the wax strips from her eyebrows.

"I was such a bitch to you," she said, her voice sounding heavy with regret. "I thought that my looks could get me everything I wanted."

"They did, Carol," I said. "You did have everything, including Colin Peters."

She looked at me from her prone position on the treatment bed.

"It might have seemed like that to you," she said.

I could see that her eyes had become glassy. Had I made the wax too hot while I'd been daydreaming, or did she really feel remorse for her actions all those years ago? I moved on to her legs and bikini line, considering her words; too late now.

"I didn't have that much really," she continued." Only my looks – and they fade don't they? Not like brains and hard work. Looks made me lazy, Lindy."

She swallowed hard and reached out, resting her hand on my forearm.

"You were the best friend I ever had and I treated you so badly. I was so mean to you. Can you forgive me?"

I turned away and reached for the mirror, unable to tell if she was being sincere.

I passed her the mirror so that she could check her reflection and my handiwork.

She moved her head from side to side, arching her eyebrows up and down and pursing her full lips.

"Thanks, Lindy." She beamed at me. "Perfect. But then I knew it would be. If you did everything here with the same attention to detail you did at school it couldn't be anything else. It's no wonder you've made a go of this place. You're very lucky."

I thought of all the nights I'd worked late, all the missed holidays to make a something of my life, all the nerve-wracking moments when I thought I'd never get any customers. Striking out on my own without someone to share it with. But then to someone like Carol who'd only ever had to rely on her appearance I suppose it did seem like luck. She'd never had to work hard – only on maintaining her appearance. It seemed ironic that I'd made my success out of looking after everyone else's.

"I used to envy you so much when we were at school," she said as she got dressed. "I envy you even more now, Lindy, seeing all this and what you've done with your life. I don't seem to have done anything with mine."

She couldn't hide the sadness in her voice and I hardly knew what to say.

"Maybe you'll pop in again sometime," I said. We walked through to the reception area.

"Yes, perhaps I will." She looked at me and seemed to hesitate. I watched as she twisted her bracelet around and around her slender wrist, her beautifully manicured nails clicking against the gold. She raised her head and was about to say something but the door opened and another client walked in. The moment was gone. She drew herself more upright, wrote out a cheque and handed it to me. "That's if I'm still around of course." She flashed me a brilliant smile. The mask was in place.

I held the door of the salon open for her and waved as she got back into her car. From the salon window I watched her drive off, before returning to the reception desk.

I picked up her cheque and studied the flamboyant signature – then tore it into tiny pieces and watched them flutter into the wastebasket. The cheque would bounce, I had known that when she walked into the salon. I had it on good authority that her husband's business was on the rocks and he'd decided to share his problems with someone younger. They'd lose the house, she'd lose her husband and, as she said herself, looks don't last forever. If she was trying to keep up appearances she was fighting a losing battle.

I looked in the diary at the rows upon rows of booked appointments, each page as full as the next and realised that I had the advantage. Keeping up appearances was my business after all.

Squirrel Training

When I first saw Steve in the garden laying down a trail of nuts I thought the stress of the past few weeks had finally got to him. That the strong, unbeaten demeanour he had presented was really a magnificent act and that he was feeling as befuddled as I was. He'd been doing it for twelve days now, slowly walking backwards along the lawn, leaving a perfect line of peanuts in his wake. And then waiting.

I began to wonder if he might have developed some obsessive compulsive disorder, or that the trail was along some medieval ley line that might attract order and normality into our lives once more. There must be a reason for it but I didn't know and he wasn't telling.

Kirsty sat at the outside table watching him, face as sour as milk, arms folded tightly around her chest; a bird with clipped wings, wanting to be anywhere but where she was. But what else could we do? Grounding her seemed the only solution.

Steve was on the path waiting for the squirrel to appear. We'd presumed it was a he and had called him Sammy, hedging our bets in case he was a Samantha and we'd inadvertently caused offence. It was odd how easily we'd fallen into a habit of censoring ourselves, trying not to say or do anything that would make Kirsty flare up in anger or shut off from us entirely. Now it seemed we were afraid of offending a squirrel.

As I watched her, folded in on herself, I was at a loss as what to do to bring my little girl back. She'd become almost a stranger these past few months, hair scraped back off her face that gave her a harsh, hardened look, and make-up so black it made her pale face paler. Where had all the softness gone? She'd lost her way and I ached for her to find it back to us. I'd searched the Internet, talked to friends, read mountains of books but nothing helped. Battle lines were formed, trenches dug.

I was horrified when the Headmaster called and asked to

see me and Steve. It was so out of character, even the Head agreed with that. Kirsty had fallen in with a bad crowd and had been caught drinking vodka on the school playing fields in the middle of the day. There then followed a litany of other misdemeanours that Kirsty had managed to conceal from us – detentions, skipped lessons, forged notes. The words tumbled around me like stones.

I place a tray of drinks on the table and pass Kirsty a mug of hot chocolate.

"I didn't know whether you'd want marshmallows so I put some on the side." I smile, not too eagerly, trying to build a bridge for her to cross but Kirsty only grunts. I rack my brains. What did that book say – be concerned but don't fuss. "I thought you'd like them," I offer again.

"I'm not a kid, Mum." She sneers as she draws the mug towards her.

That was debateable but I bite my tongue. No use making things worse than they already are. Her face was pinched with cold and her hands were like alabaster.

"Why don't you get a coat? You must be frozen."

She shot me a withering look and I retreated behind my metaphorical wall. We sit in silence, watching Steve, waiting for the squirrel to make its appearance.

And before too long it does, leaping from a branch to the fence then scampering across the lawn. It stops momentarily, wary, its head to one side, then advances slowly before taking a nut between his paws.

Steve takes his mug, cupping it in his gloved hands.

"Aren't you fed up yet?" I ask.

He takes a sip. The steam rises in front of his face.

"Not really. I find it fascinating."

Each to their own, I think, but wonder if it's his way of coping, doing something to take his mind off things he can't control.

"What do you want it to do once you've tamed it?"

He frowns. "What do you mean?"

"Are you going to get it to do tricks?"

He shakes his head then blows across his mug to cool his tea.

"I don't want anything from it. It's just exciting, watching it come closer."

"They have fleas, you know," Kirsty says sulkily.

I turn to look at her. She is wary too, cautious like the squirrel, slowly advancing forward.

"Do they?" It was news to me and I wasn't about to challenge it.

"Saw it on *Autumnwatch*. That Michaelawoman got bites."

I see the chink of light and am blinded by it, afraid to say or do the wrong thing. I consider carefully for a moment.

"My dad used to say they were rats with tails."

Kirsty nods. Perhaps Chris Packham said that on *Autumnwatch* too, perhaps not, all I know is that suddenly, curiosity is getting the better of her.

"Did you learn to do that from a book, Dad?"

He shakes his head. "Just wanted to see if I could. Sometimes it's fun to have a go at things because…"

"Because what?" She is waiting. Waiting for the right answer. I swallow hard to release the tension that has collected in my throat.

Steve looks at me, then says gently to Kirsty, "…because I can."

Sammy inches forward and sits watching us, eyes bright, then gingerly selects another nut, putting it to his mouth before moving to the next one.

We are still as statues.

"It's only three nuts away now," I say in a loud whisper. Steve's fascination is beginning to rub off on me.

"Yes, us three nuts," says Kirsty. A smile breaks on her face like sun shining through storm clouds. In that brief instant I feel a door has been opened and realise that I've been looking for answers in the wrong place. Sometimes answers can be found in books but sometimes you have to rely on instinct. We all have to find our own way in life, give things a try. Sometimes it works for the good and sometimes not. I smile at Steve and know that we'll find our way, somehow – us three nuts together.

On the Beach

"Jason said I looked just like Nicole Kidman. Can you believe it?"

Sarah shook her head, her eyes fixed to the computer monitor.

I could barely concentrate on work, I was so excited. Jason reminded me of Enrique Iglesias, darkly tanned and those beautiful big brown eyes that made my knees go wobbly every time he walked into the office. "We're going to the beach on Saturday," I chirped, leaning back in my chair.

That made Sarah sit up. She stared at me, eyes popping, mouth open, jaw dangling.

"He's taking you on the beach – are you mad? The forecast's for a heatwave." She leaned forward across her desk. "Don't you remember what happened last time?"

How could I forget? I'd ended up with skin as red as my hair.

"A momentary lapse," I said. "I'll be prepared this time. I've got plenty of suncream, my floppy hat, and I'll cover up as much as possible."

Sarah laughed. "I don't think he'll be too happy about that, Kate. He's not taking you to the beach to build sandcastles. He'll be wanting to check you out in your bikini." She rolled a Malteser across the desk to me. "I don't know what you see in him anyway. He really loves himself."

"I'm sure he's really nice once you get to know him," I said, thinking of his big brown eyes that reminded me of chocolate buttons. "And I intend to do just that."

Sarah sighed and went back to her work. She had a point. It wasn't the best place for me really, not with my red hair and pale skin but I'd waited so long for him to notice me that I wasn't going to quibble over where we went on our first date. And after all, I do have my little routine: slip, slap, slop. As long as I stick to that I'll be okay. I've had it drummed into me since I got badly burned one summer when I was out playing with my friends. My mum had slathered me in factor fifteen but it wasn't enough. Ever since it had been the old Australian routine, you know the one, slip on a T-shirt, slop on some sun screen, slap on a hat.

He picked me up at ten on Saturday. The sun was already beating down on us as we drove to the beach. It only took ten minutes but even with the windows and the sun roof open it felt decidedly steamy in there. He kept shouting at the other drivers, calling them idiots, moaning at the queues. It wasn't what I'd expected.

He pulled in the car park off the promenade then turned and smiled at me and I forgot all about his bad behaviour.

"I'll park the car, babe. Do you mind getting the ticket?" he said, flicking of the engine.

"Course not," I said. We were here at last. No traffic, just a beautiful day ahead of us. I sauntered to the ticket machine, a smile as big as a Cheshire cat until I saw what they charged. "Seven pounds fifty!" I muttered under my breath. If it had been me and Sarah we'd have parked in the cheaper car park further away and walked. Still, he had driven us here. I walked back to Jason. He was leaning against the car, his face tilted up to the sun. As I handed him the ticket he clasped my hand and squeezed it.

"You're a star," he murmured.

My knees went to mush.

I reached inside the car for my beach bag.

"What do you need all that for?" he pumped the key fob and locked the car. "Surely you only need a towel?"

"You might because you're lovely and brown," I said. "But if I don't cover up I'll be smothered in freckles in half an hour. That's what you get with red hair – pale skin and freckles."

He held my chin, lifted his Ray-Bans and looked into my eyes.

"Your freckles look wonderful to me," he crooned, his voice like honey.

It made me forget all about the extortionate price of the ticket.

We started for the beach.

He held out his keys, sunglasses case, mobile phone, wallet and body oil.

"Do you mind carrying these? I don't want to spoil the line of my trousers."

I could see why. They were a bit tight, and white does get grubby so quickly if you're having to put your hands in and out of your pocket. I had room in my bag, and it really was no trouble.

We stepped onto the sand. I headed towards a space against the beach wall and started smoothing out the towels I'd brought. Jason stood surveying the beach.

"Not there, babe. Too shaded." He pointed towards the jetty. "Over there," he said. "That's more like it." He set off towards the centre of the beach, no shade, not a windbreak in sight. I watched him flick out his towel then beckon me over. I gathered together my bag, my towels, wide brimmed hat, all the things I'd carefully set out, and stumbled over to him. The sand was hot and stung my feet.

I sat down and struggled discreetly out of my dress whilst Jason stood up and peeled off his trousers to reveal the skimpiest Lycra trunks I'd ever seen. He made a big performance of stretching his arms wide and flexing his legs as if he was getting ready to run a marathon. Everyone was looking at him. A warm tingle rushed through my body. To think that he'd chosen *me*. I could almost feel waves of envy from the girls around us.

He lay down on his back, propped himself up on his elbows, looking about the beach over the lenses of his designer sunglasses. I reached for my suncream and held it out to him.

"Would you mind rubbing this on my shoulders?"

He pushed his glasses on to the top of his head, looked at the label, then passed it back.

"Sorry, babe, can't do. It's factor thirty. If I get that on me it'll mess up my tan."

"I've got wipes," I said, rummaging in my huge bag. They

were in there somewhere.

"No. I really don't want to risk it." He relaxed back onto his elbows. "You don't mind do you?"

I didn't know what to say. I did mind, I minded like crazy. But, well, it was early days, wasn't it and I didn't want to make a bad impression.

I contorted myself into a pretzel, eventually managing to get the factor thirty in most places and settled back to enjoy the sun.

Jason set the bleeper on his watch.

"What's that for?" I asked. "Do you need to go somewhere?"

He laughed, then in all seriousness said, "I set it for every thirty minutes. That way I get even coverage. Half an hour, front, back and both sides, then I start all over again." And with that he lay down on his stomach to soak up the rays.

I tried to find out about him, the real Jason, just to prove to Sarah that he was really nice, deep down – that he was as gorgeous on the inside as he was out. But after a few grunts in reply Jason said he wasn't really in the mood for talking. He said he liked to think when he was among nature. Just enjoy the beauty of his surroundings. I liked that. I made a mental note to tell Sarah on Monday.

So I left him to think and flicked through my magazine. It was getting really hot and still more people streamed onto the beach. Two girls wiggled over to where we were, one of them looking decidedly like J-Lo, her teeny white bikini setting off her deep tan, lush brown hair cascading about her shoulders. Lying on the beach must be their full-time occupation. They came and stood by Jason, shielding their eyes, looking for a spot on the overcrowded beach. It must have cast a shadow over him because he sat up.

"Move over a bit, Kate. Let's make room for these girls shall we. We mustn't be greedy."

They giggled. I peered at them from under the brim of my hat, smiled sweetly and shuffled close to Jason.

"No, the other way." Jason grinned. "There's more room

beside me."

Not from where I was sitting there wasn't.

I moved up a bit, a very small bit, and they squeezed in next to Jason.

Jason's bleeper went off and he turned on his side, back to me, facing the girls.

What could I do without making a scene? I went back to my magazine. The sun was directly overhead now and my skin began to tingle.

I nudged Jason. "I'm really thirsty. Shall we go and get a drink?"

"Not for me," he said without moving. "I'm cool."

I was melting.

"Well, I'm going to get an ice cream or something." I was loathe to leave him there, alone, after trying so hard getting him to notice me. "Come with me."

"We'll lose our place, babe." He sat up a little. "You go, I'll keep this spot. Okay?"

"Okay," I said, trying to keep my voice light. I didn't want the girls to see I was bothered – after all, he was with me. I got up and found my purse.

"Seeing as you're going anyway will you get me a bottle of water, iced, if possible? That would be sooooooo nice." He pulled down his glasses slightly and winked at me.

And I melted even more.

Up on the promenade my heart sank. The queue was a mile long, I'd be there ages.

I stood there for what seemed like years then, ice cream and water in hand, purse shoved under my arm, I headed along the prom back to Jason. The ice cream began to dribble down my arm in the heat and I licked it up.

I stepped back on the beach, inching through the crowds of sun worshippers, trying to find him and having no success – until I spotted him, rubbing suncream on Miss Fake J-Lo's back. She was giggling and making groans of appreciation.

The ice cream continued to dribble, the sun beating on my shoulders. I needed my sun protection. I could feel my skin burning and a fire welling up from deep inside. I'd had enough of the sun and more than enough of Mr Chocolate Button Eyes.

I passed him the water and he smiled appreciatively then lay back down again without a word. I sat for a while finishing my ice cream and tried to think of a dignified exit. As I popped the little end bit of cone in my mouth I had my eureka moment and got up and started gathering my things, rolling up my towels and stuffing them in my bag.

Jason sat up and flicked imaginary specks of sand off his arm in disgust.

"What are you doing?"

"I've got to go," I said, smiling sweetly. "I've remembered something."

He didn't seem bothered, just lay back on his towel. "See you Monday," he drawled.

"Yeh, see you," I said. "Looking forward to it."

"How I managed to hold myself together to get off that beach I'll never know," I told Sarah in the lift on Monday morning.

"What, you just left him? Without a fight? Without a tongue lashing?"

I nodded. We strolled across to our desks and got ourselves settled. She was still bewildered.

"That's not like you," she said, flicking on her monitor. "What was it you remembered?"

"Two things," I said, plonking my bag on my desk.

"One was my self-respect."

She leaned forward, a puzzled look on her face. "What was the second?"

"That I had his car keys, wallet and phone," I said placing them on the desk. "Oh, and these." I held up his pristine white trousers and Sarah fell about laughing, tears rolling down her cheeks. "Like I said, I'm really looking forward to seeing him.

Jam and Cheese

The jam's mouldy. Removing the lid, ready to spread it on my croissant I am greeted by a skin of grey, fluffy bobbles. I turn up my nose and sigh. Another disappointment.

"What is it?" David is spreading his toast with butter, his knife dancing across the surface.

I show him the jar, hold it under his nose. He peers in, then leans back.

"Ugh. Throw it away," he says in disgust. "I'll have marmalade." He gets up and starts rummaging in the cupboards, flinging doors open in quick succession, barely looking inside them.

"No need," I say, picking up a teaspoon. "It'll be perfectly okay when I scoop off this skin. Underneath will be fine."

I blame it on my mother – don't we always. Much maligned as we women are. But she was of the 'make do and mend' era, brought up in the war years when waste was seen as defeat. I've been thinking of her a lot these past few weeks. Wondering what she'd advise me to do if she were still here.

"Like cheese," I say.

"Pardon?" David frowns as he returns to the table, placing a jar of marmalade between us.

"Cheese," I repeat. "If it's mouldy you can cut off the bad bits and the rest is quite safe to eat."

He nods but I can tell he's not interested. I watch him smear marmalade on his toast and wonder if I should have stayed at home and let him come alone. It was a bad idea but stubborn as I am I didn't want to waste all the money we'd already paid out. Just because we're travelling together and sharing an apartment we don't have to spend all the time in each other's company. We don't have to speak.

Besides, I don't think you can claim on your holiday insurance for your husband having had a fling with his secretary – especially as it was seventeen years ago. All these years I'd lived with the understanding that our relationship was rock solid and now I'd discovered my marriage had foundations of sand.

He screws the lid back on the marmalade jar, finishing with a strong turn as is his habit. He has beautiful hands, strong and safe. Hands that caressed someone other than me. I feel sick at the thought and begin to clear the table as a distraction to send my thoughts on another route than the one it wants to follow. I don't want to go there. I run warm water into the sink and open the window. Voices from the streets below sail upwards, women talking rapidly, laughing, complaining. I plunge my hands into the hot water and just stand there, listening, thinking.

Oh, I know it was years ago but that doesn't make the betrayal hurt any less and I needed to get away from all the naysayers and friends with good intentions trying to help me decide what the best thing was for me. But how could they – I didn't know what was the best thing for me. I didn't know who *me* was any more. I'd been deceived, duped and it hurt. How it hurt.

"Do you want me to dry?" David is beside me. He holds a tea towel expectantly, waiting for permission. I want to laugh, when did he ever need permission? I can't bear to look at him at the moment. Don't even want him beside me. That close. I shake my head and he drops the towel with a sigh and walks into the sitting room.

So, what am I doing here? What is the matter? I needed space to gather my thoughts and Spain was as good a space as anywhere. Away from a British winter that had dug its heels in, just as much as his betrayal had burrowed into me. Would spring ever come? For me? For England? Here in southern Spain the air was warm, the days brighter and lighter.

I look around the room, then through the window. All of a sudden I feel stifled, unable to breathe. I need to get away.

"I'm going out. For air." I don't look back, just grab my bag. I'm out, down the stairs, heading for Marbella old town.

I browse in shops, then sip strong coffee at a small cafe off the main square where I watch the world pass by. Waterfalls of bougainvillea cascade from balconies, startling fuchsia against white walls and soft guitar music drifts from inside darkened interiors.

This I do for four days. I've no idea what David does during this time, I don't really care.

On the fifth day David comes and sits down beside me, sheepishly placing a bunch of keys on the table.

"I've hired a car for a few days," he says. "Thought we could explore a little."

I glance over his shoulder. A waiter heads towards us. It sounds tempting. It would be nice to see more of Spain.

"Apparently, out into the mountains there's the equivalent of the Lake District." He pulls a napkin from the box on the table and begins rolling it. "I thought you might like to take a look."

I sip my coffee. We won't have to speak any more than necessary.

"Why not."

I leave a couple of euros on the table and follow him to the car.

We drive along the winding roads that soar up into the mountains in silence, among golden fields, the earth baked red. Rows of olive trees stand among the hillside like soldiers and then suddenly through the curves, there's the blue of the lakes sitting like sapphires in the burnt dry earth. My heart lifts. The air is filled with the scent of wild rosemary and thyme that populate the byways – an aromatherapy treatment for free. We pull into a small car park and walk along beside the railings.

Families are picnicking among the trees, children jumping off the rocks into the water, squealing with delight. Through the pines I glimpse pedalos and kayaks and am filled with a desperate urge to be on the water.

We make our way down a windy footpath among the rocks. It's steep and David holds out his hand to steady me but I ignore it. I don't want his help and he lets his hand drop and carries on to the water's edge.

We watch a couple in a pedalo, kids jumping off the slides on the back, young families. We were like that once. Perhaps that was when he had his fling.

"Want a ride on a pedalo?"

I shake my head. I don't want to sit side by side. We've done enough of that.

David slips off his shoes and T-shirt and wades into the water. I watch as his arms spread wide and he leaves the shore behind, and then I wander over to the kiosk where the kayaks are rented out.

A dark skinned girl with a money belt chats idly to the boys that come down to the water. She laughs, tossing back her long, black curls and they jostle for her attention.

"How much for a kayak?" I ask.

"Twelve euros," she says in broken English. The youths stand back.

"I'll take one."

I hand her the cash and she finds a seat for me, hands me a paddle, then leads me to the water's edge. She selects a kayak, fits the seat in place and gestures for me to get in. I wriggle into position and she pushes me out into the water.

I haven't done this in years and it takes me a minute or two to find my rhythm, then I push away into the main body of the lake. The familiar dip and scoop as I move from the shore is soothing and powerful. Soon I am pushing hard into the water and skimming across the lake to the bays and coves; the splash of the water a welcome relief from the midday heat. I thrust the paddle hard into the water and hold it steady to turn the boat. I'd forgotten just how much I know. It's peaceful, alone.

The cliffs soar above me, people scramble across the rocks. Some wave from a cafe in the distance. The world seems full of colour out here, brighter, sharper somehow. Three children dash along the water's edge, a little black terrier running beside them barking with delight. The sun warms my back and I can feel it loosening my muscles. The water laps at my kayak. Perfection. I half turn, wanting to say: 'Isn't this wonderful?' But there's only the lake and the sky. For a while longer I wait, staring. Staring but seeing nothing.

I turn back, and make towards the girl and the kiosk. A hundred metres away I sit for a while, again, watching, drifting.

Families sit among the slopes, sharing picnics, admonishing children, lathering them with suncream, teasing, loving, caring. I lift my face to the sun, dip my hand into the lake, wipe my face with clean water. My skin feels taut as it dries. My kayak is drifting slowly but steadily back to shore.

I dip my paddle once, then again until I am in the shallows. I look back at the way I've come, all the way back.

I hear the sound of something behind me and the kayak wobbles a little, as he, David, my husband comes alongside, his hand firm as he touches the kayak, not me.

"Any room for a passenger?" David asks tentatively. His skin is tanned by the sun, his hair bleached in just these five days.

"Get a paddle from the girl." Calmness has settled upon me. "I'll wait."

"I didn't know you could do this so expertly," he says as he comes back to me.

"There are lots of things you don't know about me," I say, matter-of-factly.

And there are. Things I did before I met David. Things I'd forgotten.

I steady the boat and he slithers into place.

We are out of rhythm. He dips as I scoop. We stop.

"Now," I command. "In. Out. In. Out." After a few false starts we are synchronised, moving in harmony once more as we slide silently over the water. We weave in and out of the pedalos and other boats and I am in control, after floundering for so long.

We dry off by the shore and gathering our bags make for the top. David stretches out his hand to mine. I hesitate then take it as the act of chivalry it is. His hand feels warm and strong and we silently ascend the slopes.

In the cafe I look out across the azure blue of the lakes, shimmering in the sunshine. We order coffee and tapas of cheese and ham. The cheese is warm, sliced thinly, and I pick it up and consider it before popping it into my mouth. You can't throw something away because there are few bad bits, you can always scrape away the bad and find perfectly good underneath.

David reaches his hand out across the table and this time I offer mine in return.

"What are you thinking about?" he asks.

"Jam," I say. "Jam and cheese."

The Little Blue Jelly Dish

"Why would anyone want to keep forty-seven brown paper bags?"

Cathy fanned them out under her face, the breeze wafting her fringe from her eyes.

Steph looked up from her laptop and sat back in her chair.

"Why would anyone want to count them?" She smiled. "You're just as bad."

"Am I?" Cathy leant against the old pine dresser that had stood in their mother's kitchen since they were small children, repository for all Mum's knick-knacks and things that 'might come in useful one day'. She wasn't sure whether it was a good thing or bad to be so like her mother in this respect. She settled on good. There was no harm in storing things that may be useful. It wasn't hurting anyone, was it?

"It's fashionable now anyway."

"What, hoarding?"

"No, it's recycling, isn't it. Saving things that might be useful later instead of clogging up landfill sites," said Cathy. "Very green. Probably the first time Mum's been fashionable in years."

"And the last," said Steph. "Trust you to put a positive slant on it, Pollyanna."

Cathy placed the brown bags back in the drawer. She could understand the clutter being alien to Steph with her minimalist flat overlooking the river – all leather and cream and a place for everything. Mum had a place for everything too. The only problem was the amount of 'everything' there was.

Cathy crouched down on her knees beside the dresser and began to pull out the contents of the cupboards below. She had wanted to do this in privacy, without the eagle eyes of Steph following her every move. Steph wouldn't understand anyway. She'd laugh and think it was another one of Cathy's crazy ideas.

"What was it you were looking for again?" asked Steph, her fingers clattering over the computer keys.

"The little blue dish," Cathy replied.

"I didn't know we had one. What does it look like?"

"Blue," said Cathy with a grin.

Steph stopped typing and looked over at Cathy, raising one eyebrow like a question mark.

"Sort of a cone shape, with a little circular stand." Cathy sat back on her heels and made the shape with her hands. "It had ridges inside where the jelly would stick, and fluted edges."

Steph's brow furrowed.

"Can't say I remember it. Sure it wasn't Gran's?"

"Positive," said Cathy, picturing the dish in her mind's eye. "It was one I had when I was little."

She returned to the cupboard and began passing silver cake knives and fish slices in fancy boxes to Steph, who sat snapping them open and shut. The shelves were full of things they couldn't remember Mum ever using: free gifts from cereal boxes; numerous plates with pictures of dogs that she'd got from saving coupons from the daily newspaper.

Steph was examining a tiny china ornament Cathy had brought back from a school trip years ago. She held it pincer like in her fingers as if it were something nasty off the pavement. "Why on earth does she keep all this stuff?" she said, handing it back to Cathy.

"They might be worth something one day, according to Mum." Cathy was reaching deep inside the dresser, sweeping into the inner recesses with her arm.

"She watches too many episodes of *Flog It!* that's her trouble," Steph sighed. "You two are so alike. You believe any old rubbish."

Cathy tried to block her out. Steph was the practical one like Dad, good at logic and numbers and not given to the fey ramblings of Cathy and their mother.

"Here it is." Cathy pulled the dish out into the light,

triumphant. "My special dish."

"That's it?" said Steph, disappointed. "I thought it was crystal, something valuable."

Cathy shook her head.

"No, it probably cost less than a shilling years ago."

She felt like a child who had discovered fairies at the bottom of the garden. She couldn't tell Steph the real reason she was so desperate to find it. She couldn't bear the dismissive looks and comments. It wasn't that Steph meant to be cruel – she just didn't understand. It wasn't just any old dish to Cathy, it was her magic dish.

Steph, plainly disinterested in Cathy's discovery, checked her watch then got to her feet.

"Is there anything else Mum needs?" she said picking over the pile of things they'd assembled on the kitchen worktop. "Fresh nighties, face cream, talc. What else did she want, Cath?"

"Nothing." Cathy swallowed hard, suddenly aware of why she had wanted the dish in the first place. Wondering if it still retained its magical properties, a tentative grasp at bringing to life memories of happier times. "She didn't want anything." Tears pricked into her eyes. Mum hadn't asked for anything and that was the trouble.

She had seemed so frail and listless these past few days, almost as if she wasn't really bothered if she got better. Her usually beloved books lay untouched on the bedside cabinet, along with her knitting and a sudoku compendium.

"In that case we'll spoil her when she gets home." Steph threw a comforting arm around her sister. "We'll fill the place with flowers and all the things she likes."

Cathy wished she could be as optimistic as Steph but last night she'd been afraid for the first time. Mum's operation was a major one but all had gone well and the surgeons were confident she would make a full recovery. Only Mum seemed out to prove them wrong. When she'd been ill before she'd been anxious to get back home to look after Dad; always agitated that he wouldn't be eating well, that he looked so strained when he visited her. But since Dad wasn't here any more, she didn't seem in a hurry to get better, let alone home.

"She's never going to get well if she doesn't eat, Steph. She's got no appetite at all and I can't tempt her with anything. That's why I wanted the blue dish, it always worked for me."

Steph squeezed Cathy's hand. "She'll be okay. She'll be itching to get back to all these paper bags and bits of string. Tell her I'm having a mad clean through and getting rid of it all. That'll get her back home before you can blink." She snapped her laptop shut and slipped it into its leather bag then jangled her keys from her pocket.

"Sorry to dump all this on you for a few days but I just have to go to this conference." She hugged Cathy and made for the door. "I'll take over when I get back, give you a rest."

Cathy waved her off and returned to the kitchen. The house was so quiet. Mum usually had the radio on for company. She began replacing the contents of the dresser until only the blue dish remained on the table. She picked it up and turned it around in her hands. How she'd loved it, her own special dish. On Sundays, after dinner, Mum would fill it with trifle and plonk a glacé cherry on the top.

"It's a sundae dish," Dad had said, spelling it out to her. "S-u-n-d-a-e."

But it was her magic dish, especially for Sundays – and all the special days in between.

Cathy remembered being off school with measles, mumps and upset tummies. Mum would make her a bed on the sofa, plump up her pillows and tuck her under the duvet so that just her head was peeking out. She'd make a quick dash to the corner shop and come back laden with Lucozade and a stack of comics – then she would sit down beside her and read.

After a while there would be chores to do and while Mum busied herself Cathy would watch the flames dance in the fire. Then out would come the blue dish filled with jelly or ice cream, or sometimes tinned fruit salad with evaporated milk to tempt her appetite back. Mum made being ill the most special time. Magical. Just the two of them.

Cathy had had to share lots of things with Steph but not the little blue dish – Mum had saved it just for her.

The mere sight of the blue glass made Cathy feel better, lighter somehow. The memories it evoked filled her with warmth and perhaps it would do the same for Mum and bring her home again. There was a chance it still contained some of its past magic – and at least they could share a few memories if not. She knew it was daft to put so much hope in a little blue dish. She was being silly. Steph hadn't remembered ever seeing it so there was no reason that Mum would. Perhaps the memories were Cathy's alone.

She boiled the kettle and rummaged in the cupboards, finding a pack of raspberry jelly and a tin of mandarin segments. She made the jelly, leaving it to set while she walked round the corner to the local store.

She'd never got the hang of making custard from scratch, not without the lumps anyway, and picked up a carton along with the cream. Thank heavens for convenience food, it was cheating but the state Mum was in at the moment she wouldn't notice, even if she did manage to eat some.

Cathy moved along the magazine racks, selecting the ones with stories in them, almost like comics for grown-up girls. She wasn't sure whether she was doing this for Mum or for herself, but she had to try something.

When she arrived in the ward her mother was propped up, staring listlessly in front of her. The TV blared blindly away, unnoticed.

She smiled weakly when she saw Cathy walking towards her laden with bags and an armful of magazines. A flicker of interest stirred in her eyes. Cathy laid her burden down, leant forward and kissed her mother on the cheek.

"What have you got there, love?" said her mother perking up a little with curiosity. "Are you moving in?"

"You'll see soon enough," said Cathy. "Now then, Mum,

up you sit."

She gently propped her mother forward, plumping up the pillows behind her. Then pulling the table towards her mother, she began to reveal the contents of her bags. She poured a small glass of Lucozade and held the glass while her mother sipped at it.

"What's in the other bag?"

Cathy tapped the side of her nose. "That's for later." Placing the glass down, she settled beside her on the bed and began to read aloud from the magazines – the gossip, the gardening, a short story or two. They discussed the fashion and the recipes and debated how complicated the knitting pattern was. Interest seemed to stir in her mother, the colour slowly returning to her cheeks.

"Oh, I did enjoy that, love," she said, as Cathy let the magazine drop to the bed. "I couldn't face reading a novel at the minute. It feels too much."

"I'm not finished yet," said Cathy leaning across to her other bag. She brought out the blue dish and set it on the table in front of her mother.

"I didn't know we still had that." Her mother's eyes began to twinkle. "Cost me sixpence that did. You used to love it when you were small. Called it your magic dish."

Cathy smiled and nodded and rummaged again in her bag.

"You used to stick your fingers in the grooves and pull up the last little bits."

"And you'd tell me off," said Cathy. "But I didn't mind. I didn't want to waste any."

Cathy flicked the cream topping up with a fork she had brought with her and passed Mum a spoon.

"You've forgotten something."

"Don't be so impatient, Mum." Cathy thrust her hand into the bag and brought out a small plastic pot. She pulled back the lid to reveal one large glacé cherry which she plopped on top of the trifle. "There you are."

She grinned like a child. "Perfect," she said and dipped

her spoon into the cream. It was a struggle but after a while the dish was empty and laying down the spoon, her mother stuck her fingers into the grooves of the dish, then licked them clean.

"How was that, Mum?"

"Delicious, love," she said, patting her mouth with a tissue. "But it could have done with proper custard." She winked at Cathy and reached out her hand to clasp her daughter's.

"Looks like your little blue dish is still magic after all."

Table for Two

Jimmy suggested Lorenzo's. I'd have chosen Pizza Hut but he said he was paying. The restaurant was busy, sleek waiters gliding among the tables. He was already twenty minutes late.

There was a commotion in the lobby, waiters bustling. Diners turned to see who required so much attention but I'd have known with my eyes shut. Jimmy liked to make an entrance.

He strode over to the table and slid into the chair beside me. He was looking good. Slim, tanned, expensive suit.

He leaned across and kissed my cheeks, clutching my shoulders, squeezing.

"You're looking wonderful, Jules. Gorgeous."

I smile, knowing he is waiting for me to return the compliment – so I don't, and it wrong-foots him. He's used to me playing the game his way.

He orders red wine, by the glass.

"Driving," he says.

I look at his face. The light in here is subdued but the lines on his face are starting to show. Frown lines, laughter, worry; they've all left their mark. I know I've not escaped the passage of time but I hope that my lines are weighted more in favour of laughter these past years, erasing the ones of grief and worry that Jimmy left there.

He reads the menu.

"What are you having?"

"Fish."

"You always chose fish." He smiles, remembering other times, other menus.

"You always had steak." And he did, nothing clever about that.

His wine arrives and we order. The waiter slips away.

He holds his glass aloft.

"To us," he says quietly.

I clink my glass to his. His cuff is frayed a little, his cufflinks the ones with paste diamonds I bought him years ago. I wonder how we stayed married so long? Why we married in the first place? Was it the triumph of hope over adversity as I liked to kid myself, or was I a prize winning doormat as my friend Natalie had so nicely put it?

He'd asked to meet me alone.

"Maybe he wants to apologise," I'd said, "for all the hurt."

"Dinner wouldn't be long enough," Natalie sniped.

I'd talked it over with Liam and he agreed it was best to go. Get closure, once and for all.

Jimmy starts to tell me what he is doing – this and that. Where he is living – here and there.

"LA, South of France. You know how it is."

Yes, I know how it is, keeping up the pretence that all is wonderful in Jimmy's little world.

"I heard you were married," he says, holding that trying-not-to-care note from his voice.

I nod. "To Liam. We have a daughter, Lucy."

"That's nice."

Nice. He's still trying to trip me up, make me feel that what I want is not good enough. Nice to Jimmy is insipid and boring but that's not how I'd describe my life – more like wonderful, huge, glorious. I have my beautiful Lucy, I have Liam, we have our home. I can sleep at night, safe by Liam's side, knowing that our bills are paid and no one is chasing us. Not having to tell lie after lie to get through each day.

Then I realise that nice is exactly what it is to him. No parties, no fast cars – or fast women. Nice is just how Jimmy would see it.

"Yes, it is nice," I say.

The food arrives. Jimmy eats with gusto, large bites, eyeing my fish. Wanting a bit of what I have too.

"You used to pass me forkfuls of what you were having. Can you remember? We used to share."

I nod, chew my food, savouring each mouthful. We never shared, I gave him mine – he ate his own. All of it.

The waiter clears the plates.

"Do you want dessert?" he asks. I sense his anxiety. He doesn't want me to go. Do I mean that much to him or is he just lonely these days? True friends are few and far between when you have money, even more so when you have none.

I shake my head.

"Coffee then?"

I can manage coffee. I've managed all these years, I can manage coffee.

Funny how all the memories crowd in. Coffees in restaurants, coffee to keep me awake juggling three jobs, coffee to keep going when all I wanted to do was give up.

We chat for a while but I realise I have nothing to say. There's nothing I want from him and nothing he can give.

He asks for the bill. I take my purse from my bag and he reaches out – puts his hand on mine.

"I'll get this."

I look into his eyes. Eyes I once searched for signs of love. I'd like to have said I found some glimmer of truth there but I didn't, just the lights of the restaurant reflected in his dark brown irises. I hesitate, his hand still clasping mine. I feel the warmth. And I remember. All the years he treated me badly, the debts he left, the tears I cried.

I close my purse, and I let him pay.

Watermelon Jones

"Do we have a name for Baby Jones yet?" The nurse laid the bundle in the crib by the bed. Liz grinned sheepishly. "We still can't decide. I'm hoping my husband's had a few ideas since last night."

The nurse took the clipboard from the end of the cot. She looked up at Liz and smiled.

"You'll think of something soon enough. She's a proper little peach." She made a few notes before returning the clipboard to its home and moved off to the woman in the next bed. Liz sat back into her pillows. Peach, plum. Why were babies described as fruit? Truth be told she'd looked more like a little prune when she was first delivered.

Liz sighed. She couldn't get Watermelon Jones out of her head. It was so distracting. Carl had named 'the bump' that. Said Liz looked like she had a watermelon shoved up her jumper.

"You might get done for shoplifting."

"Thanks a bunch."

"Well a watermelon is far nicer than a football." He'd gently rubbed her extended tummy. "It's a good name, Watermelon Jones, got a nice ring to it."

Liz had giggled.

"I suppose if pop singers and movie stars call their kids Apple or Peaches we could plump for Watermelon."

She'd clasped her hand over his, brought it to her face and rubbed her cheek with the back of his hand.

"Bit of a mouthful really and not sure that that would go down too well in the playground in a few years' time. It's all right for Hollywood but I don't think Bournemouth is quite ready for Watermelon Jones."

Liz had carried the baby all on her front. From the back she didn't look pregnant at all.

"Bound to be a boy," said her mum. "Girls lay all round, boys are all at the front."

"It's the other way around," said Gran. "And a better way

of telling is to get a key on a piece of string and dangle it in front of your bump. If it goes clockwise it's a girl, anticlockwise it's a boy. Foolproof."

Liz shuffled over to the edge of the bed and looked at her little watermelon.

She lifted her up and snuggled her close, pulling the blanket away from her tiny face. She deserved a name. The little scrap couldn't stay Watermelon much longer – it was embarrassing.

She glanced at the ward clock. Visiting time. Carl would be here soon. Hopefully this time they could agree on something suitable for Baby Jones.

She wasn't normally prone to dithering but it was such a momentous decision. The name they gave their child was going to stay with them all their life and Liz didn't want her daughter to go through the teasing she'd had at school.

She'd had hated them all. Thin Lizzy, Busy Lizzie, Dizzy Lizzy, Lizzy Dripping. She hated Beth, insipid – and Betty reminded her of elderly aunts with pink twin sets and matching pearlised lipstick that lingered on the end of their filter tips. And her surname, Mickleburgh, was even worse. No one could ever pronounce it correctly and she was tired of standing at desks, school or reception, and having to spell it out. It was a relief to marry Carl. There was no way you could make mistakes with Jones – and Carl be it with a K or C couldn't really be shortened or punned upon. That's why she'd liked Adam if it had been a boy. Simple, uncomplicated. But they couldn't agree on a girl's name. They'd deliberated for months and in the end they'd decided that once the baby was born they'd find a name to fit.

Her mother had said she knew she was an Elizabeth as soon as she had looked at her.

"You looked like an Elizabeth."

"Whatever an Elizabeth is supposed to look like," said Liz.

"Like you of course. Just like you."

It's a good job she did – the other name that had been

standing by was Astrid. It didn't bear thinking about.

The doors to the ward swung open and the visitors filtered in. Proud dads and grandparents with face-breaking smiles; little boys and girls coming to meet their new brother or sister. And then she saw Carl – or rather she saw a huge bouquet wearing his jeans walking towards her. He lowered the bouquet and grinned, then seeing she had the baby in her arms, placed them on her table.

"Hello, Mrs Jones," he said leaning across and kissing her. "How's my little Watermelon today?" he stroked the baby's cheek with his finger.

Liz was overwhelmed with the flowers.

"They're absolutely gorgeous."

"You two are worth it. Not every day a man gets himself a beautiful daughter to match his wife."

He took the baby in his arms and Liz leaned across the bed to admire the bouquet.

"Any ideas?" she said.

"What about Melonie?"

Liz didn't want to laugh. They began the guessing game again.

"Evie?"

"She doesn't look like an Evie."

Carl looked around the ward for inspiration. His eyes fell on the bouquet.

"We could call her Rose, after Mum?"

Liz looked at her precious bundle; she would do anything for Carl.

"Sorry, Carl, nothing personal, I love your mum to bits but this little one really doesn't look like a Rose."

Carl peered at the baby, swaddled in the hospital blanket. He looked to the bouquet again.

"Iris?"

Liz screwed up her nose.

"Doesn't really go with Jones does it. Too maiden aunt-ish."

Carl pulled at the bouquet. "I know, Lily, Fern,

Gypsophila."

The two of them burst into laughter.

"She is a little flower and no mistake," giggled Carl. "But I can't imagine her called any of those."

He handed the baby back to Liz.

The baby blinked and wriggled her little hands, trying to break free of the blanket. Liz looked at her baby and then to Carl. Plain Carl Jones, the most loving, generous man a girl could wish for. He was calm, practical, uncomplicated – would their beautiful daughter be the same?

Liz sank back into the pillows reflecting on those heady days when she fell in love with him. He made her feel like a princess doing the most simple, everyday things. And suddenly she knew exactly what to call Baby Jones.

She smiled at him, satisfied she had the answer.

"Carl, can you remember our first date? You didn't have any money and so we strolled down to the river and had a picnic."

Carl squirmed. "We can't call her squashed tuna sandwiches."

Liz chuckled. "Not that, you daft thing. That was the day you gave me my first bouquet."

Carl tilted his head back, trying to remember a bouquet. He shook his head. "I didn't give you any flowers."

"Yes, you did, love. We sat by the riverbank and you passed me flowers – and we made a daisy chain."

Liz stared intently at their child. Innocent and uncomplicated – just like a daisy.

"Daisy?" Liz felt the word roll around her mouth. Baby Jones looked up at her, blue eyes blinking, then gave a windy smile. Carl reached out and clasped Liz's hand. The nurse came to the bed, admiring the flowers.

"Did you bring a beautiful name in with this gorgeous bouquet, Daddy?" she asked Carl.

"Sort of," said Liz, grinning broadly. "Nurse, say hello to Daisy Jones."

Jumpers

Gabby slid back the wardrobe doors and took a deep breath. This wasn't going to be easy. She'd been dreading it but Mark said it was best to get stuck in and get it over with. She had promised her mother and she wasn't about to let her down.

It felt strange being in her mother's house knowing that she would never be back, never shout upstairs that tea was ready or to tell Gabby to 'turn that blooming noise down'.

Rain hammered on the windows and ran down the glass like tears. It had rained when they'd said goodbye to Mum. Gabby turned away and began hauling the clothes off the rails, throwing them onto the bed.

What was she supposed to do with a lifetime of fashion?

"I want you to go through it all, Gabs," her mum had said. "If you can sell some on eBay and make a pound or two great, but if not take it all down to Oxfam. Someone will be glad of it and I won't be needing it any more."

"Don't talk daft, Mum," Gabby had insisted. "Come the winter you'll be the first one pulling on your cardigan."

Joyce had reached across and grabbed her daughter's arm, squeezing it firmly to make Gabby see that she was serious.

"I won't, love. I won't have need for any of that any more. Please do this for me."

And Gabby had promised. Who was she to argue with her mother's wishes?

She began sorting through clothes her mother had accumulated over the years. Pulling out a shocking pink flying suit Gabby began to wonder if her mother had kept everything she'd ever worn. She held it up to herself in the mirror and pulled it across her waist.

"Mmm, very Anneka Rice."

Gabby spun round. Mark was standing in the doorway, smiling, keys in his hand. "Just off to fetch the kids from school, will you be okay?"

She nodded. It was something she'd rather do alone anyway. He'd been a fantastic help with the rest of the house but sorting Mum's personal things was something she needed to do by herself.

Rummaging in the back of the wardrobe Gabby retrieved a pair of check Audrey Hepburn pedal pushers Joyce had stuffed there long ago. A huge smile crept over her face. Gabby examined the back – and the huge tear at the seam. Mum had been in the playground at the time. Gabby had been pushing Sean in the baby swing and Joyce had been gripped by a sudden urge to go on the slide. She chased up the steps like a child but as she stretched out one leg to get seated there had been an enormous ripping sound and Joyce had exposed her big flowery knickers. Gabby was only too grateful Mum hadn't been wearing a thong. They had giggled all the way home, a lime green fluffy jumper tied around Joyce's waist to cover her embarrassment. That was Mum all over, spontaneous and fun. How she missed her.

Gabby began to pull trousers, skirts, dresses off their hangers and folded them into bin liners. Then she started on the drawers. Mum had loads of sweaters. She'd always felt the cold and never went anywhere without a sweater or cardigan – even in high summer.

"You can't rely on the English weather, Gabs. Well, I suppose you can," she added sagely. "You can rely on it to be unpredictable."

Unpredictable, just like Joyce.

Gabby took out a horrendous bright blue sweater with apples, cats and alphabets knitted into to it. She cringed as she remembered going out with Joyce when she was wearing it – well, that and the bright orange angora with the green trim came a close second. She was glad to see the back of them and stuffed them quickly into a bag.

Her fingers found the baby pink cashmere. Joyce's favourite sweater – and Gabby's. Light, warm, and knitted to last a lifetime. Gabby remembered happy times, snuggling up to her mother when she was wearing it, munching away on hot buttered toast and watching *Coronation Street* together. It had been darned so many times, no one would possibly want to buy it. Gabby lifted it to her face and rubbed it on her cheek. It smelt of Mum, it felt like Mum. She couldn't give that away no matter what. She put it on one side. She'd take that one home.

She sighed heavily and carried on, putting the last of the items into bags and taking them down to the hall.

She was sitting at the table sipping coffee when Mark came back with the kids.

"Finished, love?"

"Yes, all by the door," she said softly. "Just as she wanted."

"Well at least that's all over," he said, putting his arm around her shoulders. "Ready to start again when we get home?"

Gabby groaned. She hated packing but it had its plus points. A fortnight in Greece beckoned and a chance to catch up with Joyce. When your mother does a Shirley Valentine, someone has to sort out all the stuff that gets left behind. Fun and unpredictable, and fed up with the cold and rain, Joyce had taken a holiday in Crete and decided to stay. A brief trip back to put her house on the market was all she could bear before jetting back to warmer climes.

Gabby picked up the pink cardigan and put it in her bag; she'd give it to Joyce next week in the sunshine.

Country Living

Karen wondered whether to tell Andy about the cow in Sheila's garden – then thought the better of it. She wasn't speaking to him anyway. When she'd first saw it she wasn't sure whether she'd had one too many glasses of wine. She'd squeezed her eyes open and shut three times but the cow was still there, eating Sheila's perfectly manicured lawn in the moonlight. She could see it quite clearly, grazing away, and watched mesmerised for a second or two before the rest of the herd rounded the corner and sauntered down the road. Karen took another sip of wine. She'd never get used to the ways of the country; it was harder than she thought, there was so much she didn't know. Thinking nothing more of it she returned to her book, *Start your own Organic Garden.* She'd read the same three lines over twenty times now but she was darned if she was going to talk to Andy. He could apologise first.

Andy, meanwhile, had contented himself with flicking through the TV channels whilst the adverts were on. Typical, she thought, he knew it drove her to distraction. She was just about at breaking point when the phone went and Andy disappeared into the hall to answer it.

He came back in, a puzzled look on his face. Karen concentrated really hard on the rogue sentence. "I've just had a really strange call from Sheila."

Karen grunted and stayed glued to the book. Sheila was the cause of their row. Sheila with her home-made jam and her country pies that she passed over the fence when we came in from work. Karen knew it was a lovely gesture and she should have been grateful but now it was getting on her nerves. It never seemed to bother Andy. He thought her apple and blackberry pies were the best he'd tasted.

"I think she must be having some sort of waking nightmare."

"Oh, you've only just noticed have you," Karen said sarcastically, making an even greater attempt to get past the line where the soil has to be turned regularly to begin with.

"No, seriously." His voice was firmer now, but agitated. "She said she's got a cow on her front lawn." He glanced at the mantle clock. "At half past eleven at night."

"Well she has," Karen said, without taking her eyes of the page. Riveting it was. She was desperately trying to get past the bit about the best time to plant runner beans but her eyes kept glazing over. "It's no big deal is it? She'll do anything to get your attention."

Andy shook his head in despair. "Karen, this *is* serious. We have to go and help. It must have escaped from one of the fields up the road. It could cause an accident." His voice was taking on a note of exasperation now.

"It's not there any more," she replied, trying to sound as if she was well used to these odd night-time occurrences. She flicked an imaginary speck off the glossy pages of her country living bible. "It joined the rest of the herd as they walked past not ten minutes ago. It probably stopped off for a snack."

Andy eyed her suspiciously. "A herd?"

"Yes. A herd," Karen replied, a note of disgust in her voice. Why could he never resist the opportunity to ridicule her and her lack of knowledge of things agricultural? It wasn't her fault she didn't know as much as he did. She'd never lived in the country before. She hadn't spent every summer holiday on an uncle's farm in some sleepy little village in Gloucestershire.

When they'd discussed living in the country Karen was all for it. A country kitchen with Cath Kidston fabrics and cream enamel pots and jugs; roaring log fires, a herb garden, Sunday lunch at the pub, plenty of space to park. She hadn't counted on the smells and the mess that go with the fields and leafy lanes or being stuck behind tractors on narrow lanes and her car permanently caked in mud. Nor had she counted on Sheila and her pies.

Karen had made an apple pie that afternoon using fruit from their own tree. Today's offering, with its beautiful sugared brown crust, looked perfect, unlike her previous two attempts – until she cut into it. The inside looked, and unfortunately tasted, like wallpaper paste. Andy suggested Karen ask Sheila her secret – she must have some tips for a novice. She'd scraped the pie into the bin and hadn't spoken to him since.

She looked at him now and wondered how he could be so insensitive. Andy leaned across her and they stared out of the window. The road was quiet and the amber street lights cast soft, cosy shadows across the hedgerows and the neighbouring cottages. He looked at her again. Karen tried hard not to be distracted by his warm brown eyes and held her ground.

"Look, I know you think I'm a buffoon, and probably had a few too many drinks – which, I admit, I possibly have, but I definitely saw a herd of cows, about twenty of them, walking down the road, clear as day. Well, clear as night," she added, since it was. "But the moon was bright and clear and I could see them, just, well, just walking, getting some exercise I suppose."

"Ex-er-cise." He enunciated each syllable with exaggerated slowness. Stretching out the words so that they played around his mouth like a tickle. Karen could see the smile twitching about his lips.

"Yes, exercise. I'm sure they must do it all the time when the roads are quiet. Must blunt their hooves or something. Like walking a dog wears down their claws."

Andy could stifle his amusement no longer and burst into laughter, his whole body shaking with mirth.

"Don't you laugh at me, Andy Prince. I know what I saw. Go out and look if you like." She threw her attention back to her runner beans. "See if I'm not right."

"I will." He pulled on a sweater and hurried down the stairs. Karen saw him emerge in the road below and followed his progress as far as she could until he disappeared out of sight. She gave a deep sigh. Why did the reality never match up to the dream? She'd pictured herself the perfect country wife, growing her own fruit and veg, baking her own bread and cakes, sewing intricate quilts to throw nonchalantly over the furniture like they did in magazines. Not that she'd ever attempted these things before when they lived in town but she'd imagined that it would all come so easy to her once she was in the right setting.

How she'd come down to earth with a bump. When she'd flung open the windows to let the fresh air sweep into the house she hadn't counted on the smell of the silage and cows and other farmyard smells. Nor had she got used to the stubble burning after harvest. Even with the windows closed black specks of dirt crept stealthily into the house and danced around in the autumn air. But worse than that, was that every time she suffered some small disaster in her attempts at country cooking, Andy would pop home with a jar of home-made pickle and a game pie from Sheila to rub salt in the wound. Why didn't he understand that it only made her feel more of a failure than she felt already?

She got up to put another log on the fire. She didn't know how long Andy would be but he'd be cold when he got in. The fire crackled and spat in the grate as flames licked thirstily around the new addition. She went back to her seat by the window. She was pleased they'd chosen a house with the lounge upstairs and the bedrooms down. It offered the most wonderful views over the countryside and she never ceased to be amazed at nature's bounty that unfolded before her. But apple pie and jam? She doubted she'd ever conquer the dark arts.

She was there for no more than a few minutes, arms wrapped tightly around her when she spied the herd rounding the corner. They ambled past the window, heads nodding agreeably followed by Andy talking companionably to a man in a wax jacket and stripy pyjama trousers. They looked up and waved. Andy said something and the man laughed and she watched them disappear down the lane.

She pulled the small sofa closer to the fire and curled her legs up underneath her. At least she had seen a herd of cows.

She was right this time. The mantle clock ticked away in the background, soothing and steady, and she closed her eyes and resisted the urge to carry on reading.

Some time later Karen heard Andy coming back into the house, the heavy thud as he shook off his boots and started up the stairs. He seemed to have gained a spring in his step. The walk must have done him good. His cheeks were red and he looked invigorated when he came into the room.

"I apologise," he said. "You were quite right."

Karen felt a wave of relief wash over her, grateful she hadn't made a fool of herself again. Perhaps she and Andy could make it up now.

"It was the farmer from Manor Farm."

"The pretty one on the left. The wonderful farmhouse with rambling roses over the front door?"

"I suppose so. It was hard to see in the dark." He went over to the fire and held his palms open to the flames. "Tom Richards, his name is. I helped him round them up. Appreciated the help. He's invited us over for dinner tomorrow – to say thank you. If you'll come with me that is?" he added gently. "You don't have to speak to me."

Karen softened, a feeling of vindication making her more receptive to his peacemaking advances.

"Someone had driven past and opened the gate," he continued. "Young lads I guess, out for a lark. But so foolish. Those cows could've done untold damage and may have had to be put down if they'd hurt themselves. Good job you saw them. Tom was so grateful."

Karen felt her cheeks slowly start to heat up.

"So they weren't exercising then?"

He was smiling now, a warm glow that lit up his eyes. "Not this time, no." He sat down beside her on the sofa. His breath was cold and fresh from the brisk walk and he smelt of night air and leaves, and fields and moonlight. He rubbed his hands together then placed one arm around her. "So we're speaking again then?"

"Looks like it."

"Sorry I made fun of you."

She snuggled closer to him, pleased that they had found a way to come together. "What were you laughing at when you walked past?"

"I was telling him about the cows' exercise and blunting their hooves."

"You didn't?" Karen pulled away from him, horrified that whole village would soon know of her ignorance. "He'll think I'm an absolute fool. I'll never be able to show my face again. I'll be a laughing stock."

"Hey, hey." He pulled her back into his arms again. "It was a joke. I told him nothing of the sort. He was laughing at what a pair we'd look if anyone saw us. Him in his pyjamas and me in my boxer shorts and a sweater. Anyone coming out of the King's Head would've thought they'd had one too many and dismissed it as a fantastically good night."

She looked into his eyes, so tender, so full of warmth and love – there was no malice, no edge of superiority to be found there. "He said to come over tomorrow, meet his family."

"I wouldn't know what to talk to them about. I don't know anything about farming."

"You could ask him about your runner beans," he said, laughing quietly. "It has to be easier than reading that book – you haven't turned a page all night.

She grinned up at him then stretched an arm around his stomach and laid her head against his chest.

"I so wanted to be the perfect country wife, Andy. I wanted to do everything right."

"There's no such thing. Don't you think that the women here go to the supermarket or farmers' market just like everyone else?" He planted a kiss on the top of her head. "I should think Sheila's one of the few women around who still makes all her own jam. But then you don't have to live in a village to do that."

Karen knew he was right. Andy had never made any requests for home-made jam and pickles or home grown veg. It was she who had put the pressure on herself. She let the book slip on to the floor and snuggled up closer to Andy. There were better things to do in the country.

Looking for Mr Darcy

"Apparently reading's the new rock and roll, Annie. Bookshops are now *the* place to meet a hot date," Carmen called to me as I finished making the coffee and came back into the lounge. She was sprawled on the sofa with her feet up, long slim legs elegantly resting on the arm of the sofa.

"Must mean that I'm in fashion then," I said, passing her a mug. "Got to be a first."

She raised her beautifully shaped eyebrows at me and went back to the magazine. I stood with her mug in my outstretched hand, waiting.

"It gives advice. You're not going to find Mr Darcy in the romance department these days, you have to go to the travel and sports sections, or, best of all, try the action section. We ought to go and have a look round."

I watched as she ran a perfectly manicured nail under the line she was reading before I gave up and put her mug on the table.

"It's only women in the romance section," she went on. "If it isn't I'm sure it's not the kind of bloke you're looking for, Annie. Bit too pink."

I sat down in the armchair opposite and sipped at my coffee.

"Not for me, Carmen. I've had enough of your madcap attempts to find me a boyfriend thank you very much. I'll stick to the heroes in my books. Less likely to break my heart."

"That's because they're not real, Annie." She swung her legs over the arm of the settee and sat up to drink her coffee. "It stands to reason doesn't it? You love books so you're bound to find someone suitable in the bookshop. Shared interests and all that."

I shook my head. "Last week you were adamant that the key to a successful romance was that opposites attract."

She plopped the magazine on the coffee table, picked up her drink and sat back into the sofa.

"Tell you what," she said, totally ignoring my remarks. "I'll meet you at that big bookshop in town on my lunch break. We can have a skinny latte and survey the talent at the same time."

"I'm not sure that's a good idea."

"What have you got to lose?" she asked. "If we don't spot any likely candidates at least you can go home with a new book – Sophie Kinsella is Pick of the Week. If I don't find you a date such is my confidence in my shy, little self that I'll buy it for you."

How could I resist?

It's not that I don't appreciate Carmen's efforts to help me find my own Mr Darcy, because I do. Maybe it's because my heart's not in the things she comes up with. It's all right for her with her Latin looks and Beyoncé figure. I have to work a bit harder than she does. Under her guidance and tutelage I'd tried the car maintenance at the adult ed, a cliché I know, but I got nothing out of that other than the fact that I'm no longer a helpless maiden and can fix my own carburettor – not a good move according to Carmen – men like helpless. I tried supermarket dating and was an abject failure among the frozen food aisles. Speed dating just made my head spin and my feet ache – everyone just looking for a quick date, not that there's anything wrong with that but I'm looking for something a lot more substantial and long term. I'm fed up with all the 'getting to know, don't like you' part. It's all a bit too contrived and I'm more of the opinion that my someone special will come along in their own good time. So I didn't hold out any hopes for the bookshop but Carmen's good fun and meeting her for lunch would break the day up for me. At least I could get myself a book to spend the evening with.

We met on the Friday afternoon. Jazz music was playing on the sound system and I could smell rich coffee wafting from the back of the shop. Carmen was by the magazines reading up on the latest gossip and swotting up on next season's 'must haves'.

I nudged her arm and she returned the magazine to the rack.

"Now, let's approach this methodically," she said.

That's a first for Carmen.

"We'll give the crime section a wide berth, obviously, and the sci-fi – can't think that you'll find anyone suitable there. Let's try the action/thriller area."

It was empty.

"Perhaps they're all out saving the world from power mad megalomaniacs," I suggested.

Undeterred, Carmen strode off to the sports section. We were in luck. As well as a few women checking out white water rafting and rock climbing there were two men browsing the shelves. One she dismissed automatically. The other seemed to meet her approval.

"What about him?" she tilted her head towards a tall, slim guy dressed in jeans with a crisp white T-shirt. He looked promising until I saw the book he was reading. I dragged Carmen away.

"What's the problem? He looked great."

"Fishing, Carmen, fishing's the problem," I said under my breath. "I don't fancy being up at the crack of dawn and sitting on a damp riverbank all day, not being able to talk in case I disturb the fish."

"At least you'd have time to read," she suggested. "Sitting cosily under an umbrella, cuddling up to him."

"I can think of nicer places to read, like curled up in a big armchair with a box of toffees and a mug of tea." I linked her arm in mine and dragged her deeper into the shop.

The computer section was full of women, as was the DIY.

"I suppose that's a sign of the times," I said sadly. "No wonder there's no romance left in life. Women are quite capable of running things themselves and don't need a man to fix things or sweep them off their feet. We're not going to find a Mr Darcy here unless it's between the covers of *Pride and Prejudice*."

In the travel department we passed a handful of students with rucksacks on their backs, and a man, whose cream framed sunglasses hung by a green string around his neck, looking at the European road maps.

"Too old," hissed Carmen. "Besides which – if you want to travel you don't want to be sat in a car for three days. He's probably got a *Reader's Digest Book of the Road* on his back seat."

I stifled a giggle.

"What about him over by the bargain books," I suggested.

Carmen gave him a brief glance.

"Cheapskate."

I surveyed him from the safety of the poster rack, he looked quite nice really, like he remembered to wash and shave, unlike some of the inhabitants of the 'heavy rock' section.

"That's a bit unfair," I said in his defence. "He could be saving money on books to spend on something else."

"Well something else is not himself," she said with disdain. "Look at him. He needs a good haircut and a new pair of glasses by the look of it. And if he won't spend on himself he certainly wouldn't want to spend it on you."

I pulled away from her in disgust.

"I don't need anyone to buy things for me, Carmen. I earn enough to look after myself. I just want someone to have fun with, share things with."

She had the decency to look suitably chastened.

I strode off to the chick lit section. At least I felt at home with Bridget Jones and her mates.

Carmen leaned with her back to the shelves, watching for a moment before shrugging her shoulders in defeat.

"It's not working is it? Let's grab a coffee before I have to go back to work."

I handed her the Pick of the Week from the display table.

"You go pay for this, I'll get the coffees," I said, and gave her my sweetest smile before skipping up the stairs to the coffee bar.

Carmen's not a reader. Not like I am anyway. She devours the gossip mags and the *OK!*s and *Hello!*s with a hunger but she's never been one for books, whereas I love reading. You can be in another world when you're well into a book. Once I was so engrossed reading on the bus that I missed all my stops and ended up at the terminus. It was a bit of a shock to find myself there actually – I was convinced I was at the siege of Leningrad. I had to wait forty minutes for the next bus home but I didn't mind. I'd nearly finished the book by the time I'd got back and could take myself to Hollywood to warm up – via the latest Jackie Collins.

As soon as I got in from work that evening I started to get acquainted with Sophie's latest characters. I'm a dab hand at cooking and washing up one handed these days. I used to read when I was ironing with the aid of a cookery book stand until I burnt a hole in my best linen blouse.

I looked forward to a long hot bath and a quiet night curled up with Sophie. And that's when the trouble started.

* * *

Carmen says I must be one of the few people who don't mind waiting in for workmen. And I don't. I settle down with a good book and don't feel at all miffed if they don't arrive on time – and the books on the shelves in my hallway are always a talking point.

Which came in handy when I met Paul, Gary, Ian and Ollie.

Paul's the carpet fitter. He's into James Herbert and Stephen King. I'm reading one of the books he lent me last week. I swapped him for a John Grisham. I'd never read any of the legal thrillers before but I got that from the insurance assessor, Gary. Nice bloke, went on about numbers a bit too much though and was keen to stress the importance of culpability just a tad too often. Ian, on the other hand – Ian's the electrician – he's a fan of Terry Pratchett and Bill Bryson. We had some rather interesting conversations as he went over my electrics on Tuesday.

None of them were like Ollie. He's the plumber – he arrived on the Wednesday. Barely reads at all. Says all he wants to do after a hard day's work is to have a good meal and then park himself in front of the TV to relax. I'm cooking him dinner tonight as a matter of fact.

He was so understanding when he came to fix the bathroom. Not like everyone else who rolled their eyes to the ceiling or laughed at my little mishap.

You see, after my trip to the bookshop with Carmen I'd become so engrossed reading that I'd forgotten I'd left the bath running until I saw the water dripping from the light fitting. By the time I'd raced up the stairs to turn the tap off the weight of the water had brought part of the ceiling crashing in onto the lounge below, drenching the sofa and dear Sophie's tale was a soggy mess. It's not something I want a repeat performance of – and I shouldn't really have to now, thanks to Ollie. He bought me this natty little gadget, an alarm to hang around the tap that goes off when the bath is full. Said he'd done it himself when waiting to find out who murdered the opera singer in *Inspector Morse*. He loves a good mystery, especially Agatha Christie's *Poirot* and *Miss Marple*. He hasn't read the books but loves the TV series and said he understood that moment of absorption only too well.

Quiet and thoughtful, that's Ollie, and darkly handsome to boot. I'm not sure what he looks like wading into the river in his clothes but I'm sure given time I could find out.

Hilary's Handbag

I've always been curious about Hilary's handbag. And I hadn't meant to be rude – I wouldn't upset Hilary for the world – I just think I was at the point where curiosity overcomes politeness because I definitely heard my mouth saying what I thought I'd only been thinking.

Hilary looked up from her coffee.

"What do you mean a woman my age?"

I had the grace to blush.

"What I meant was," I took a deep breath, choosing my words with more care this time. "I thought that by the time a woman got older she could make do with a smaller handbag."

You see, Hilary's not one of those women who could get by with one of those chic little handbags people carry around these days, you know the pastel leather or straw ones with bamboo handles, or those quirky ones made out of old cigar boxes, or even a sensible leather one. Hilary's handbag is, well – big – enormous even. Made of blue patchwork, edged with sequins, a bit of braid here, a strip of velvet ribbon there. Fascinating. Well to me anyway. Just like Hilary really and it's intrigued me ever since I first met her.

I'd signed up for a course at the community centre down the road 'Writing for Pleasure and Profit'. It was the profit bit I was interested in. At least it offered some chance of earning me something in between making fruitless trips to the job centre. Hilary was there, sitting across the table from me, her bag on the desk in front of her. I was enthralled. I'd never quite seen anything like it, a kind of Mary Poppins portmanteau and, each lesson, when I was supposed to be listening, I would wonder about what it contained.

When the course ended we began to meet in the cafe at the new shopping centre. We'd be there for ages – at least two large skinny lattes and a strawberry cheesecake. My hubby, Pete, wondered what we ever found to talk about all that time but I loved Hilary's company; we would laugh about the daftest things and I always felt cheered after our meetings. All my worries and problems seemed to melt away in her company.

"Well," I went on, trying desperately to explain myself. "When I was a teenager I never needed a handbag. A lipstick, tissue and a couple of pound notes stuffed in my jeans and I was alright. Then I met Pete and I had to buy a handbag, to carry his wallet, keys, cigarettes and lighter – until he gave them up because I was pregnant with Melanie and he didn't want to harm the baby."

She let me gabble on, a bemused expression upon her face, obviously thinking I was quite deranged. A young woman struggled by with a pram laden with carrier bags, right on cue, which nicely illustrated my next point, and we moved our chairs in to help her get past. She smiled her thanks and we carried on.

"Then of course I needed a bigger bag because of all Mel's paraphernalia: dummy, change of clothes, spare nappy, toy to keep her amused. Now she's fifteen and using her own jeans pockets – only it's a tenner she carries and a mobile phone – and…" I held up my canvas handbag. "I can carry a smaller bag but you've still got a huge handbag, Hills – and I don't understand why."

I peeled the cellophane off my sandwiches and began to eat.

"This old thing," she said with wry amusement. "I've had it years, got it when we were on holiday in Devon. The kids were with us then so you can tell how old it is. We were strolling through one of those quaint little villages, the ones full of thatched cottages. You know the kind I mean?"

I nodded and chewed whilst she went on.

"A woman was making them in her shop, beautiful they were, all different colours. Bit expensive but you could tell that woman really loved what she was doing." She patted it affectionately. "Yes, a lot of love went into making that handbag." She hesitated for a moment and then said, rather generously I thought, after all I haven't really known her that long and it was rather nosey of me to say the least. "I'll show you if you like."

She moved our coffee cups to one side, plonked the bag in front of her and began to reveal its contents.

"Purse." She laid an old battered wallet style, red leather purse, bulging with receipts in front of me, smoothing it lovingly with her hand. "Harry bought it for me when we went to Paris for our twenty-fifth wedding anniversary. Never been abroad before." She closed her eyes and stopped for a moment to savour the memory. I pictured her with Harry in some cute little cafe, sipping black coffee, watching the world go by. "Spectacles." She made me jump. "Spare spectacles in case I misplace the first pair…"

She shook them in front of me and we both laughed and then she continued. "…cheque book, tissues, pair of tights, car keys, mobile phone, bit of make-up, needle and thread, small torch, screwdriver…"

"Screwdriver?"

"Well, you never know when you might need one do you?"

"Don't suppose you do," I mused. "Must remember to get one myself." I swallowed my disappointment. I thought she would have had something really intriguing in there for the size it was. But a screwdriver?

She rummaged around in the depths of her bag then grinned at me like a mischievous child.

"And my blessings."

"Your what?"

"My blessings," she repeated, although she knew I'd heard her the first time.

She placed a blue velvet drawstring bag on the table and returned the rest of the contents to her larger bag which she put on the chair next to her.

I know what you're thinking. I was too.

"What are blessings?"

"They're the little bits and pieces I keep with me to while away the time when I'm in a traffic jam, or in the doctor's waiting room or, well, just feeling a bit sorry for myself."

I could never imagine Hills feeling sorry for herself, she just wasn't that type. In all the time I'd known her, she'd always been positive and upbeat, never complaining. I envied her her good spirits and wished I could be more like her.

She pulled apart the drawstring, delved inside and handed me a photograph. An old black and white. A couple standing with their arms around each other.

"Your parents?"

"That's right. Taken just before my dad was killed in the war. I was seven at the time."

"You must have missed him terribly," I say, which seemed so inadequate in the circumstances. I give it back to her and as she looked at it her smile became as warm as the sun beating down on us through the glass windows of the cafe.

"I did. I often wondered what life would have been like if he'd been around but I had the most wonderful mother. The best anyone could wish for. I've been very lucky."

She followed it with pictures of her husband, Harry, her boys, Mike and Nick. We ooed and ahhed over pictures of her grandkids. Then she passed me a small pink band encased in plastic, a regular, everyday hospital identity bracelet.

"That's from when I was in St Mary's. A few years back now."

I read her name on the strip, now a little faded with age and much handling.

"From when you were pregnant, Hills?"

"No. I had cancer. They removed the lump. I'm alright now. Lucky, you see."

"Oh, Hills, I didn't know." I felt embarrassed now at how I had intruded on her private world and wished I'd never opened my big fat mouth.

She reached out and held my hand.

"No reason why you should, love. It was a long time ago and I've been perfectly healthy for years now, but when I hold that little piece of plastic I remember how precious life is and how I nearly lost it – and it makes sitting in a traffic jam seem nothing at all."

The child in the pushchair began to grizzle and the mother gave it a bottle that had been warming in a container. It immediately quietened and started to guzzle away greedily. We both smile at her and she shrugs her shoulders and uses the break to drink her own coffee.

Hilary was still peeling things from the small bag. She unfolded a scrap of paper and handed it to me.

"It's the poem, 'Warning'. You know the one about wearing purple and a red hat that doesn't go."

I grin and sip my coffee.

"*I shall go out in my slippers in the rain…*" I quote.

"*And pick the flowers in other people's gardens,*" she continues, "*and learn to spit.* I quite fancy having a go at that."

Mischief dances across her face. I can just imagine her doing everything in that poem, or at least having a go. She refolds it and puts it back inside the bag.

"Reminds me to enjoy my old age – at least I'm here and I'm going to have fun doing lots of things I never dared to when I was younger." She leans back in the chair. "There are a lot of my friends that haven't been so lucky, Julie, so it's no good grumbling about the bad things old age brings like wrinkles and aches and pains. Old age is a gift like everything else."

She moved back toward the table.

"Couple of notes my kids wrote me when they were small. Harry and I waited so long for kids we thought it would never happen, then, just like buses one came along straight after the other." She gave me a couple of sheets of well worn paper folded into quarters covered in childish, uneven handwriting.

"I was nearly thirty-five when I had my first. I know it's not old these days but trying is different to deciding not to have any or putting it off until later."

She puts the precious treasures back into the velvet bag.

"So you see, Julie, I like to count my blessings, not just in my thoughts, but with these things to remind me in my little bag. It soon cheers me up if I'm feeling a bit of a misery."

The child starts to cry and whimper. We watch as he upturns his bottle and shakes it, trying to figure out where all the milk has gone. His mum has nothing else to give him and rummages around in her holdall. Whilst she is preoccupied, obviously looking for that elusive toy or pacifier, Hilary delves into her bag and pulls out a red tube. I am at a loss as to what it is. And then I see. Hilary unscrews the top and blows gently into the hoop. A stream of small bubbles bounce around in the air and pop on the outstretched hand of the toddler sitting spellbound… and quiet. Much to the relief of the young woman. She gives Hilary a grateful smile.

And that expresses everything I know about my friend, Hilary. It's always smiles all round. I don't think there's a place she goes that she doesn't leave happiness in her wake.

She drains her cup and replaces it on the saucer and puts her 'blessings' in her handbag.

"Thanks Hilary," I say.

She looks across at me, puzzled.

"For what, love?"

"For showing me that there are so many blessings in my life that I don't ever stop to take stock of."

"Comes with age, me dear," she says in a silly voice.

She stands up and holds out her arm for me to hook mine through then picks up her bag from the table.

"Come on, my girl, let's go get you some bubbles."

"And a bag for my blessings," I add, excited at the thought. "Let's make it a big one."

ABOUT THE AUTHOR

Tracy's short stories have been published all over the world in magazines like *Woman's Weekly*, *My Weekly*, *Take A Break*, *Best* and *The People's Friend*. A regular speaker at writing festivals, she also judges short story competitions and organises creative writing workshops.

She lives in Dorset with her husband and springer spaniel, both of whom are hyperactive and hard work. Her children live close by, too close really, but it does mean she's regularly invaded by the grandchildren. Cupboards are now filled with fun-size apples and Pom Bear crisps and the thought of running out of Weetabix doesn't bear thinking about. Tracy is quickly discovering that grandchildren are the perfect excuse to stop cleaning, but not writing.

Tracy finds sanctuary from all this chaos in a collection of undisclosed cafes – a skinny latte in one hand and a large piece of carrot cake in the other. She's come to the deluded conclusion that the skinny latte balances out the indulgence of the cake.

To learn more about Tracy, go to **www.tracybaines.co.uk**

Printed in Great Britain
by Amazon